The
HEADLESS HAUNT

ALSO BY JAMES HASKINS

The March on Washington

Black Dance in America
A HISTORY THROUGH ITS PEOPLE

Black Music in America
A HISTORY THROUGH ITS PEOPLE

Black Theater in America

The HEADLESS HAUNT
and Other African-American Ghost Stories

collected and retold by JAMES HASKINS

illustrated by BEN OTERO

HarperCollins*Publishers*

I am grateful to Kathy Benson, Deborah Brudno,
Ann Kalkhoff, and Pat and Fred McKissack for their help.

The Headless Haunt
and Other African-American Ghost Stories
Text copyright © 1994 by James Haskins
Illustrations copyright © 1994 by Ben Otero

Library of Congress Cataloging-in-Publication Data
Haskins, James, date
    The headless haunt and other African-American ghost stories / collected and retold by
James Haskins ; illustrated by Ben Otero.
        p.   cm.
    Includes bibliographical references.
    Summary: A collection of ghost stories and anecdotes that are part of the folklore of
African Americans.
    ISBN 0-06-022994-2. — ISBN 0-06-022997-7 (lib. bdg.)
    1. Afro-Americans—Folklore.   2. Ghost stories.   3. Tales—United States.
[1. Folklore, Afro-American.   2. Folklore—United States.   3. Ghosts—Folklore.]
I. Otero, Ben, ill.   II. Title.
PZ8.1.H267He   1994   93-26223
398.25'08996073—dc20   CIP
                                                                          AC

Typography by Christine Hoffman
1   2   3   4   5   6   7   8   9   10

First Edition

CONTENTS

The
HEADLESS HAUNT

INTRODUCTION

Most of the stories and ghostly experiences in this book have been told many times and have been heard by many people. They have become part of a folklore shared by African Americans everywhere. They are called African-American ghost stories, but they are not necessarily African-American inventions alone.

Like African Americans, African-American ghost stories have a mixed heritage. They have some roots in Africa and some in America. Especially in the case of African-American folklore it is hard to say what came from Africa, what came from Europe, and what was a result of the combination of both. Part of the reason it is hard is that the same or similar beliefs associated with death and the spirit can be found in different cultures.

Another reason is that a wide variety of beliefs can be found within the same broad culture. This is especially true of Africa, a huge continent with thousands of groups of people and languages. These various groups hold a range of different beliefs, so it is hard to say that any one thing is an "African" belief.

However, a few general things can be said of African beliefs in ghosts and the supernatural. Africans who came to the New World believed in several types of spirits. Nature spirits were the true spirits and inhabited trees, rocks, and rivers. In West Africa it was the custom to place shiny objects on trees so as to attract spirits to come and guard against evil.

Animals had spirits. Houses could also have spirits. Houses were protected from evil spirits by specially carved door locks or posts carved with fertility symbols or other images.

Then there were human spirits—not just one spirit per person, but at least two. One was the soul, or dream soul, that existed before, during, and after bodily life. Another was the bodily spirit. Usually, a child was given two names—one for the bodily existence and one for the dream soul.

It was believed that the dream soul, especially, could be good or evil, depending on how it was treated. For that reason, funerals were very important. Unless a dead person was given a proper funeral, the dream soul was prevented from associating with other spirits and would be doomed to wander the face of the earth forever looking for a final home. It would return to haunt the remaining members of the family and make their lives so miserable that they would wish they were dead themselves. The ghost would also do evil to any other human being who happened to get in its way.

Africans and Europeans had some similar ideas about souls. Both believed in eternal souls and the possibility of spirit journeys. Though Europeans believed in a single, evil, powerful Devil, Africans did not; however, many African gods had evil and dangerous ways. Europeans believed that the spirits of the dead could make themselves known in the form of ghosts, while Africans believed in the "living dead," which we call zombies.

As Europeans and Africans came together and shared their cultures, each borrowed from the other. As the population in power, European culture was more often imposed on Africans than the other way around. But in the case of folklore, including ghost stories, the sharing may have been quite equal. After all, slave women often reared white children, and when they were small the children of both races often played together. In most cases what makes these stories African American is that they have been told by African Americans.

We are lucky also that we have some firsthand accounts of African Americans' beliefs about ghosts and spirits. In the 1930s members of the Georgia Writers' Project interviewed blacks in that state. These recorded interviews give a good idea of how strongly some older black people in Georgia believed in ghosts sixty years ago. But it is hard to say how many of these stories are real memories and how many are just good stories. Chances are at least some of the elderly subjects were just trying to please their eager interviewers. And perhaps some of them deliberately made up stories as a joke on those eager interviewers.

Most of the ghost stories and ghost experiences in this book are fifty years old or more. For a time it was hard to find a good new ghost story—either made up or actually experienced.

Ghost stories are fun—both to tell and to read or listen to. The good ones survive for years, passed down from generation to generation. And lately there seems to be a new interest in them—not just in the old ones but also in new ones. Like horror movies, they can make us shiver and squirm, and then make us laugh at ourselves for being scared. As the tales in this book prove, some of the best ghost stories come from that combination of African and European folklore that is called African American.

Ain't I Got to Believe?

As for ghosts, ain't I got to believe in them? Why, I can see them myself. You see, I was born with a double caul over my face, and anybody knows that a person born with a double caul over their face can sure see ghosts. There's more than one kind of ghost. Some come before you natural and pleasant; then some can sure make you scared. I can tell long before anything happens when it is going to happen. Nothing ever happens to me without me knowing it long before it comes.

Aunt Mary Hunter
Old Fort Section
Savannah

WHAT IS A GHOST?

A ghost is the spirit of a dead person. When the person dies, the spirit remains. Sometimes the spirit begins to separate from the person even before the person is dead. The spirit appears to a loved one, or calls the loved one's name, and that is the sign to the loved one that the person will soon die.

Ghosts take many forms. To most people, ghosts are only a puff of steam or a gust of warm air. Sometimes they look just like the shadows of the people whose spirits they were. Or they may take the form of a cat or a dog, or another animal.

There are many terms for a ghost in African-American folklore. One is haunt, usually pronounced "hant." The difference between a ghost and a haunt, according to some traditions, is that a ghost is male and a haunt is female. But sometimes you hear about a "he haunt," so that isn't always so. Other types of ghosts are plat-eyes and jack-o'-lanterns.

WAIT TILL EMMETT COMES

Once upon a time an old black preacher was riding his horse to a church he served at some distance from his home. Night fell and he could not find his way in the dark.

After a while, he saw a light and made his way toward it. He found that it came from a small cabin. He got off his horse, tied the horse's reins to a fence post, and knocked on the door. When the man who lived there opened the door, the preacher asked if he could spend the night.

"Well, Parson," said the man, "I certainly would like to help you out, but my cabin has only one room, and I have a wife and ten children. There just isn't any place for you to stay."

The old preacher leaned up against the side of the house and sighed. But he slowly untied his horse and mounted him, preparing to ride out into the night.

Just then the man in the cabin stopped him. "You might sleep in the big house," he said. "There's nobody in it and the door isn't locked. You can put your horse in the barn and give him some hay, and then you

can walk right in. You'll find a fireplace in the big room, with the wood all laid for the fire. You can just touch a match to it and make yourself comfortable."

So the old preacher decided he'd do just that. But as he and his horse disappeared into the darkness, the man called out, "Parson, one more thing. I ought to tell you, that house is haunted."

The old preacher hesitated for a moment. Then he said, "Well, I guess the Lord will take care of me."

Arriving at the big house, the old preacher put his horse in the barn and gave it some hay. Then he walked over to the house, and sure enough, he found the door unlocked. In the big room he found a great big fireplace with the wood all laid and ready to kindle. He touched a match to it, and in a few minutes there was a roaring fire. He saw an oil lamp on a table nearby and lit it; then, drawing up a big easy chair, he sat down to read his Bible.

After a few hours, the fire had burned down to a great heap of red-hot coals. The preacher was still reading his Bible when he heard a sudden noise in the corner of the room. Looking up, he saw a big, black cat. Slowly stretching himself, the cat walked over to the fire and flung himself onto the bed of red-hot coals. Tossing them up with his feet, he rolled over in them. Then, shaking the ashes off himself, he walked over to the old preacher and sat down beside him, near his feet, and looked at him with his fiery green eyes. He licked out his long red tongue, lashed his tail, and said, "Wait till Emmett comes."

That made the preacher nervous. But he decided the best thing to do was go on reading his Bible. So he did.

A little while later, he heard a noise in another corner of the room, and looking up, he saw another black cat, big as the biggest dog you've ever seen. Slowly stretching himself, the cat walked over to the bed of coals in the fireplace, threw himself into them, tumbled all around, and tossed them with his feet. Then he got up, shook the ashes off, and walked over to the old man. He sat down at the man's feet opposite the first cat. He looked up at the man with his fiery green eyes, licked out his long red tongue, lashed his tail, and asked the first cat, "Now what shall we do with him?"

The first cat answered, "Wait till Emmett comes."

The old preacher was beginning to get scared. But he thought it best to continue reading his Bible, which he did. In a little while, he heard a noise from a third corner of the room—a third big black cat. This one was as big as a calf. He came slowly out of the shadows, stretching, walked slowly over to the fireplace, and jumped in. He rolled over and over on the coals, tossed them with his feet, took some into his mouth, chewed a bit, then spat them out. Then, shaking the ashes off himself, he walked over to the old preacher and sat down right in front of him. He looked down at the man with his fiery green eyes, licked out his long red tongue, lashed his tail, and said to the other cats, "Now what shall we do with him?"

The other cats said, "Wait till Emmett comes."

By this time, the old preacher was scared to death. Trembling, he slowly closed his Bible, put it into his pocket, and rose from the big easy chair.

"Well, gentlemen," he said, "I certainly am glad to have met up with you this evening, and I surely am pleased to have had your company. But when Emmett comes, you tell him I have been here and gone!"

WHO CAN SEE GHOSTS?

- *All animals have "second sight" and can see spirits.*
- *A baby born with a caul, or veil, over its head can see ghosts. The caul is a portion of the membrane that surrounds the fetus in the womb. A baby born with a double caul over its head is also believed to be able to see the future.*
- *A baby born in the breech position, or feet first.*
- *A baby born with a hole in the lobe of the ear. It is called a "ghost lobe."*
- *A person whose eyebrows meet.*
- *A person born on Christmas Day.*
- *The seventh child born in a family.*

It Vanished Like a Shadow

One night I finished eating dinner. Then I walked to the kitchen door. I saw a strange man coming down the road; he was about twenty yards away. I turned my head to look in the house, and when I looked back, he done disappeared. I know he must have been a ghost.

Another time I heard a knock on the door. I heard it three times: Bam! Bam! Bam! When my dog heard that knock, he hollered like he was scared to death. I got up and went to the door and my hair raised up on my head. When I got to the door, I saw something as big as a cow, only it looked like a dog. Then it vanished like a shadow.

Henry Bates
Currytown

THE DESERTED VILLAGE

There was once a black village in West Texas that had about two hundred families. But then a ghost in the shape of a cat arrived. It had two heads and eight legs. It went to everybody's house all the time. At first it was a helpful ghost. The crops were fine, and folks could harvest two or three bales of cotton per acre. The people thought the ghost was bringing them good luck. When it came to their house, they would feed it and tell it when they wanted rain, and the rain would come.

One day a girl caught a little dove and put in it a cage. The ghost came that night and said, "If you don't let that fowl out, you'll die on the third day."

The girl didn't let the dove go, and sure enough, on the third day she died. After the funeral was over, the ghost came and stood on her grave.

Then all the townspeople decided to kill the ghost. They went after it with dogs, guns, and horses. The dogs tracked it and caught it. But before the people

could get there, the dogs let the ghost go. It never came back. But the next day all the crops were eaten by ants, and in a year's time there were no more than three families living in that town. And they were all white.

LITTLE NERO
AND THE MAGIC TEA CAKES

When Little Nero was not more than five years old, his mother was killed in an automobile accident. His father took the little fellow to live with Little Nero's grandmother, Old Lady Coleman, and paid her for his room and board. Old Lady Coleman loved the little fellow very much, because he was her only grandchild. She did everything under the sun to please him. She got him lots of toys to play with. She got him a little red wagon to ride in, a little red rocking chair to rock in, and a cute little bed with a feather mattress to sleep in.

The only thing Old Lady Coleman wasn't very good at was cooking. Little Nero had a real sweet tooth and liked sweet things to eat all the time. But it didn't matter how many sweet things Old Lady Coleman cooked for him—lemon pies, chocolate cakes, sweet-potato pies, peach cobblers—he would not eat more than two bites of them. He'd just sit around with his hand under his chin, looking out the window and daydreaming.

Old Lady Coleman couldn't figure out what was wrong. She coaxed him to eat her cakes and pies, but he just wasn't interested.

Then something happened to change Little Nero's eating habits. One night at about twelve o'clock, Little Nero felt something real hot, like a wind blowing in his face. That woke him up. Then he saw a white puff of smoke coming through the window. When it reached his bed, it turned into a white dog. That white dog kept coughing up little tea cakes onto the floor. Once it had coughed up a goodly pile of tea cakes, it turned back into smoke and went back out the window.

Little Nero was scared, but he did like the looks of those tea cakes. He jumped out of bed and started eating

them. After eating about fifteen or twenty, he was full. But there were still more on the floor. So he went to the kitchen and got a flour sack and put the leftover tea cakes in it and tucked the sack of tea cakes under his mattress.

The next morning, when Old Lady Coleman came into Little Nero's room, he jumped out of bed and acted so happy that she wondered what had come over him. She said, "Nero, I'm sure glad you are feeling so good this morning. How come you're so happy?"

Little Nero didn't say a word. He just took his grandmother by the hand, lifted up the mattress, and showed her the flour sack full of tea cakes.

"Where did these tea cakes come from, Nero?" she wanted to know. So Little Nero told her what had happened during the night and then grabbed up a handful of tea cakes and started eating them.

Old Lady Coleman was glad Little Nero was happy, but she doubted his story. Pretty soon, though, she started to believe him, because it didn't matter how many tea cakes he ate during the day, the next morning the flour sack would be full again.

One time Little Nero's father came to see him and took a peek at the tea cakes. Then he exclaimed, "That's the same kind of tea cakes the little fellow's mother used to cook for him all the time."

The Ghost in Black Silk

When I was just a young boy, my family used to live in Currytown. Me and my brother used to go and see my aunt who lived in Yamacraw. To get from our house to where she lived, we had to go past a cemetery which was in back of Union Station.

One time we had been to see my aunt and it got to be late. We started for home. It was the beginning of night. My brother had rheumatism, and he was hobbling along on a stick. We started along by a fence to get to West Broad Street, and when we had gone about a hundred yards we saw a lady coming toward us. She was very fair skinned, and she was all dressed in black and had on a long black veil. Her dress was black silk and rustled as she walked.

My brother and I, we were surprised to see the lady all of a sudden, for we hadn't noticed her before. She came up to us and said, "Are you going round the fence?" We told her we was, and she said, "You're not afraid?" and we said, "No—we're not afraid."

The lady wanted to walk with us, and we all start

walking along. We had gone a short ways when all of a sudden we looked in the cemetery, and we saw a little white thing rising up out of the ground. It was kind of hazy and shadowy, and it sprang up from the ground and streaked out to meet us on the path ahead. It looked like a little animal.

The lady, when she saw the little white something coming, she darted out like lightning and went right to meet it. When she got to it, she disappeared right into the air, disappeared right before our eyes. My brother forgot he was crippled—he dropped his stick and started running, and I ran too. And we never stopped running, kept right on going until we got home to Currytown. He doesn't like to speak of it today because we're not superstitious.

James Collier
Brownville

HOW TO ACQUIRE THE ABILITY
TO SEE GHOSTS

- *Punch a hole in your earlobe and create a "ghost lobe."*
- *Look back over your own left shoulder.*
- *Look through the eye of a needle.*
- *Look through a mule's ear.*
- *Look into a mirror with another person.*
- *Break a yellow-billed cuckoo's egg into some water and then wash your face with it.*
- *Wipe off a dusty nail and put it in your mouth.*
- *Break a stick in two.*

If these simple methods don't work, try these more elaborate rituals:
- *Go to a graveyard at noon or midnight with a mirror and a pair of new steel scissors. At exactly twelve o'clock hold the mirror up in front of you and drop the scissors on the ground. The scissors will cut away your doubts and fear. Then call out the name of the person you want to see, and that person will appear in the mirror.*
- *Put six pure-white dinner plates on the table and then go to the graveyard at twelve noon and call the name of the dead person. The spirit will answer at once.*

THE GHOST LOG CABIN

In a remote and lonely spot three or four miles from town stands an age-worn and weather-beaten log cabin that for miles around has long been famous as the birthplace and residence of all the ghosts in the neighborhood.

Although it is worn and run-down, it is still livable, and sometimes when men are caught out late on hunting expeditions, they are tempted to spend the night there. But the stories about it usually make them think better of that idea.

Occasionally a man will decide that the stories are nonsense and enter the cabin, hoping to spend the night. But they are always frightened out of their senses about midnight by a loud rumbling and by deep groans, and in a few minutes they are out of there, running for their lives.

One man who'd had such an experience was once telling a group of friends about it. "I don't believe there is a man under the sun who could stay in that cabin from darkness to daylight," he said.

"Yes there is, too," piped up one of the group, who was known as Uncle Sam. "If you'll give me fifty dollars, a chunk of bread, a frying pan, and all the meat I can eat, I'll stay there."

Taking him up on the dare, the others gave Uncle Sam all he asked for. Carrying the money, bread, frying pan, and meat, he set off alone for the cabin. He entered the old building, started a fire in the fireplace, and just before midnight, the time the ghost was supposed to appear, he began to fry his meat. He then lit his pipe, found an old chair to sit on, crossed his legs, and waited for the meat to be cooked.

Suddenly a small, black, formless creature about the size of a rabbit ran out on the hearth, spat across the frying pan into the fire beyond, and turned to Uncle Sam.

"There is nobody here but you and me tonight," it said.

Uncle Sam saw it, but at the same time he didn't see it. He heard it, but at the same time he didn't hear it.

He was too busy watching that the meat was frying properly.

The ghost spat again on the fire, this time about an inch from the frying pan. This made Uncle Sam angry. "Don't you spit on that meat," he cried, making for the little creature.

Then as quick as a flash the ghost kicked the pan of meat into the fire, clawed Uncle Sam between the eyes, and sat down on the hearth.

"There's nobody here but you and me tonight," it said again.

Now Uncle Sam was scared. Trembling from head to foot, he arose and stammered, "I-I-I'll not be here long." He then made a beeline for the door.

Thus Uncle Sam joined a long line of men who tried, and failed, to spend the night in the ghost log cabin.

UNCLE HENRY
AND THE DOG GHOST

One Saturday, early in the morning, Uncle Henry Bailey left Clarksville to go down to the big baseball game and barbecue they were having down in Oak Grove. Uncle Henry used to pitch for the Clarksville team, and he still liked to see a good baseball game. That day the Knights of Pythias and the Odd Fellows were playing off a twelve-inning tie from the Saturday before.

Uncle Henry reached Oak Grove long before the game started. He got himself a good seat on one of the wagons that was standing at the far end of the pasture where they were having the barbecue and ball game. Pretty soon the players on both sides came loping up on their horses. They tied their horses to a fence post, went over to the barbecue pit, grabbed a big hunk of barbecue, ate it, and after resting up a bit, started to warm up for the game.

But they were real late getting on with the game after all, because one of the pitchers who had to come from way off somewhere reached Oak Grove about an hour late, and this moved the starting time of the game way back. But Uncle Henry didn't budge until the game was over, and by then it was pitch-dark. The last train for Clarksville had left, so the only way Uncle Henry could get home was to walk.

Uncle Henry didn't mind walking in the daytime, but he did not in any way relish walking down the railroad track in the dark. What bothered Uncle Henry was: How was he going to see where he was walking, as dark as it was? So he stooped down and picked up a Coca-Cola bottle that was lying on the ground beside the wagon he'd been sitting on and went to the grocery store, which was still open, and bought enough kerosene to fill up the bottle. Then he took off his necktie, folded it up, and stuffed it down the neck of the bottle of kerosene. He struck a match to it, and as soon as it started burning, he began walking down the railroad track toward Clarksville with the lighted Coca-Cola bottle in his hand. It was getting darker and darker all the time and looking stormy, too, so Uncle Henry got real scared and imagined he saw all kinds of eyes shining up at him from beside the railroad track. He finally got so scared, he started running. He was going just like old Engine Number 30 headed north, and before you could say Jack Robinson he had reached Annona. But when he reached it, he stopped dead in his tracks, because standing right in front of him was a

great big white dog with red eyes. The longer Uncle
Henry eyed the dog, the bigger the dog got.

"Get away from me!" yelled Uncle Henry, hitting at
the dog. When he did that, he knocked his necktie out
of the Coca-Cola bottle and onto the ground. Now he
couldn't see a thing. So he started running down the
railroad track again, with the big dog right at his heels.
Faster and faster Uncle Henry's feet carried him toward

Clarksville until he finally reached his house and fell onto the porch limp as a dishrag and just panting for breath. His wife, Aunt Jenny, heard him fall on the porch, so she fetched an oil lamp off the kitchen table and went out to the porch to see what was the trouble.

When she saw Uncle Henry stretched out on the porch, she ran into the house and brought him a dipper full of well water. He drank it, and pretty soon he sat up and told Aunt Jenny all about the dog running him all the way home from Annona.

Aunt Jenny listened to Uncle Henry, and when he was finished, she cracked her sides laughing. "Henry, come to think about it," she said, "you don't have to run away from that dog and think you were a goner. That dog spirit was just some good Christian friend who came back from the grave to bring you good luck and protect you on the way home."

Uncle Henry was awful sorry that he had run himself nearly to death for nothing. The dog spirit didn't make Uncle Henry stop going to ball games, but he never did stay away from home until dark anymore.

I Was Born With a Caul

I was born with a caul. That means I see ghosts. At least I could see them until after I stopped having children. Then I stopped seeing them.

Three of my children were born with cauls, too. They were always more scared than the others. They were always afraid of the dark and never liked to go off by themselves. I never knew just what they saw.

Ghosts look just as natural as anybody. Most of them ain't got no heads. Just go right along down the path. One time I saw a man go right down that path there. I went out to see who he was and all of a sudden he disappeared. There weren't any foot tracks or anything. I never saw him again. I think maybe he was guarding buried treasure.

Another time I looked out in the yard and there was a hog just eating up the corn. That was the biggest hog I ever did see. He stood there and kept eating and eating. I ran and told my husband, and he dropped what he was doing and came running. When he got there, the hog had disappeared. There wasn't a sign of him, and the corn was all right there. It didn't look like anybody had been eating it at all. Then one time I saw a crowd of cows in the field. There was a big bull in the middle. They were just cutting down the corn. There was a big empty space where they had already eaten. I ran to where my brother was and told him to come quick. We ran where the cows were, but when we got there they had all vanished. They were all gone. There were no tracks and all the corn was grown back. All of a sudden I felt a terrible pain. I could hardly get to the house. That's the way it is about the spirits. If you tell that you see them and they disappear and no one else can see them, then it causes you to get sick.

Liza Basden
Harris Neck

PLAT-EYES

Some unfortunate spirits who have not been properly buried become plat-eyes. Originally, the plat-eye, which had one eye that dangled from the middle of its forehead, was a particularly evil form of ghost. But the term plat-eye has come to be used to describe an evil spirit of just about any form whose purpose is to guard buried treasure.

DADDY AND THE PLAT-EYE GHOST

Hattie, Maizell, Sin-Sin, and the rest of the kids standing under the pine tree hollered at Raisin to come over. She knew they were going to work her over about ghosts.

"A plat-eye ghost's gonna get you, Raisin," said Sin-Sin. "Plat-eye ghost's gonna come in your room, hop on your back, and ride you all night long, just like you was an ole mule. You be thinking you're having the horriblest dream, but it'll be that old plat-eye riding you."

"I ain't scared of nobody's plat-eye," Raisin said. She crossed her toes inside her shoes, just in case. "And I bet you never even seen one, neither."

Ursula hollered that her daddy had. "And it had big red eyes. Daddy saw it on Cypress Swamp Road just about night when he was a little boy. He say he and some other guys were walking back from fishing in the creek—the part that's up around Cypress Swamp Cove where those condos are now. Him and his uncle Toe and them.

"He had left his knife back at the creek where they'd been fishing. He decided to go back to get it. The others went on. He had a bucket half full of fish, too. But Daddy say he went back through the swamp grass along the edge of the creek and found his knife. It was moonlight out, see, so he didn't have no problem.

"On the way back he kept thinking something was following him, but when he would look around, he wouldn't see a thing. Just as he got onto the bridge over the creek, he felt his back start to get real hot right under his shoulder blades. He said it was like two pins were being burned into his back. He said when he jumped to one side, he looked back and saw two huge round eyes red as blood and with steam rising from them hanging in the air not two feet behind him. He started walking backward from those eyes, trying not to look into them, because a plat-eye can suck your breath out if it can catch your eyes and hypnotize you. Still holding on to his knife in one hand and the bucket in the other, he lit out across that bridge and didn't stop until he caught up with Toe and them.

"But you know what? All the fish in his bucket was gone. Daddy said that plat-eye got 'em."

TWO BOYS AND A PLAT-EYE

Once there was a man who was mysteriously killed. Instead of being given a proper burial, his body was put into a hastily dug hole, and no preacher—not even a church deacon—prayed over him. So the man's homeless spirit became a plat-eye.

Late in the afternoon one day, a mother sent her two boys to buy the week's groceries.

Before the two boys set off on the old mule, their mother gave them a warning: "There's gonna be a young moon tonight. You take care that you get home before it shines and sets the spirits to walking."

"Yes, Mama," said the boys as they started off.

At the crossroads store, the boys bought rice, sugar, coffee, and flour. Those were the only things their family did not grow in their garden or raise in their animal pens. They put these things in paper bags and put the paper bags in a big sack. Then they climbed up on the mule's back and started home.

The mule was old and lame, and he was walking slowly as the boys started back along the lonely wooded road. The sun went down and the young moon came up. The boys could barely see, but the old mule knew the way.

But suddenly the old mule's ears started to twitch and his tail started to switch. And when the animal came to the spot where the man had been killed, he stopped and would not budge.

The boys got down and the older brother took his stick to the mule. He hit him on his side and hit him in the head. But the mule just snorted and would not move.

Then a warm gust of air passed over the boys' faces and a small white cloud floated by. It smelled like smoke from burning sulfur, an acrid odor that burned their noses.

The boys got scared. The hair on their heads stood up straight, and they shivered in the warm night air. The mule shivered, too. And then with a hoarse *hee-haw, hee-haw*, he leaped backward, throwing the groceries off his back.

Suddenly the old lame mule was running like a yearling. It was all the boys could do to catch him and scramble up on his back. He made it home in minutes, then fell down on his stomach in the yard and lay there all night, gasping for breath. As for the boys, it took their mama a long time of comforting before

they were able to go to sleep.

The next morning, mother and boys and old lame mule went back for the groceries, still lying where they had fallen in the road through the woods. There was no plat-eye 'cause plat-eyes hide in dark places when the sunlight comes.

Soon everyone for miles around had heard about the boys' meeting up with the plat-eye. That Sunday the preacher devoted his sermon to the need for proper burials at all times.

Sometimes They
Come in a Whirlwind

I've been ridden by witches and seen a thousand and more ghosts. I see them most anytime. They just float along about two feet from the ground. Sometimes they come in a whirlwind.

One day at the rosin yard there come up a whirlwind. I saw a big white man in it. I showed him to the other men, but they don't see him. I can see him because I was born with a double caul and feet first. That gives you the power to see them. A ghost comes here every night and peeps in the sewer over there. He looks in the sewer, walks to the corner, and then disappears. Any night I'm on this stoop I can see him.

Moses Brown
Tin City
Near Savannah

A NIGHT AT PICKEY'S

One evening a man we'll call Homer was walking
home from the mill with a bag of freshly ground
cornmeal. On his way he had to pass by Pickey Bailey's
old run-down farmhouse.

Pickey Bailey was a hermit who had lost both his
wife and son. Folks said he was crazy, but Homer never
had any trouble with him. In fact, Pickey Bailey usually
never even said hello when Homer passed by.

But this evening Pickey said to Homer, "Come in
here and sit."

Now Homer wasn't too keen on
going into Pickey Bailey's
house, but he was tired
and the sack

of cornmeal was heavy. Besides, a light rain was falling. Homer figured he'd rest on Pickey's porch until it stopped.

No sooner had Homer reached the porch than it began to pour.

"See that flash then?" said Pickey. "That was lightning striking my barn again."

"I didn't see a flash," said Homer. But Pickey went on talking.

"Barn gets struck about once a week and burns down to the ground. But when I go milking the next morning, it's done built up again, so I don't worry none about it."

"Well, I declare," said Homer, for sure enough the barn had turned into a charred ruin.

Just then an old blind goose came up onto the porch and began to peck at Pickey's sleeve. "She's eating corn," said Pickey. "This here's Rosemary. She's twenty-five or thirty years old. I killed her once, but it didn't do no good. She don't do nothing now but pick grass and squawk and eat corn off my coat sleeve."

"Well, I do declare," said Homer.

The rain continued to pour down in buckets. After a while, Pickey said, "You'd best pass the night here."

Homer was not looking forward to spending the night in Pickey's old broken-down house. But he couldn't go out in that rain. He followed Pickey into the dirtiest house he had ever seen.

"Want to see the parlor?" said Pickey, and not waiting for an answer, he escorted Homer into the front room. "'Twas just here my son Leslie's casket set," said Pickey.

Homer tried to concentrate on why the blazing fire in the fireplace wasn't giving off any heat.

"Never have to kindle that fire," said Pickey. "It just builds itself every twilight and goes out before day. And I never even need to clean the ashes out. Nice, ain't it?"

"I reckon so," said Homer, thinking maybe he should have gone home after all.

Pickey led him upstairs to one of four bedrooms. Homer figured it was just above the parlor where Pickey's son's casket had been. The hinge on the door was broken. He noticed another door over near the window. The knob was gone, and it looked as if it had been sealed up a long time.

Pickey lit a kerosene lamp for Homer and put it on a table by the bed. Then he got Homer a gallon of raw corn liquor. "You may need it," he said. "Good night, and I get up at five."

Homer pulled the quilt up around him and reached over to turn down the wick in the lamp. But before he could do so, the lamp went out by itself. Too tired to be scared, Homer went to sleep.

He awoke suddenly when he felt the quilt creeping down toward the foot of the bed. The lamp lit itself low, just enough for Homer to see a creature sliding in over the windowsill.

In the dim light, Homer realized it was a cat. "Howdy," it said. "I'd sure like a drink from that jug." Since he didn't see a bowl, Homer poured some of the corn liquor on the rug. The cat lapped it up.

"Are you a ghost or a haunt?" Homer wanted to know.

"Ghost," said the cat. "Haunts are female."

"Who are you?" said Homer.

"None of your business," the creature responded. But it came close to Homer, as if it wanted to be petted. "Nice kitty," said Homer, reaching out his hand.

"Leave go of me," it yelped, and jumped over the sill into the dark.

The rain had stopped by this time, and the room was very quiet, but Homer couldn't fall asleep. He lay there thinking about cats and wondering why Pickey's was so different. Finally he got tired of thinking. "Go on out," he said to the lamp, and it did.

Homer was just about dozing off when he was startled by a tapping from inside the closet. Then a voice whispered, "Get in here and make me a fruit pudding. I'll tell you how."

Homer sat up in bed. "Are you a ghost or a haunt?" he wanted to know.

"I'm a lady haunt," came the answer.

"Pleased to make your acquaintance," said Homer.

"Get me a witch doctor to help find the key to this door," the lady haunt said.

"Well, I'll look for one," said Homer wearily, easing himself out of bed.

"I'm cold. Get me a shawl," the lady haunt said next.

"Quit pestering me!" yelled Homer.

He listened for an answer, but none came. After a time the voice from the closet said, "I hope you sleep well."

"Sleep well!" he yelled. "Will you show me a man, white or black, on top side of this earth, who could sleep well in this haunt-ridden, nerve-tormenting spot? Barns burning down, cat ghosts slipping under the sill, covers creeping away, lamps going on and off, and a whiny, pesky woman in the closet!"

There was no reply.

Homer had given up on the idea of sleep by now. He went over and sat by the window and thought about ghosts and haunts. He had met one of each that night, and he realized they were just as different as regular people. The ghost was rude and the haunt was pesky.

When the sun came up, Homer decided it was time to go home. He tiptoed down the stairs. As he passed the parlor, he looked in at the fireplace. Sure enough, just as Pickey said, there wasn't an ash in it. Pickey could not have gotten up to clean it. Homer could hear him snoring in the back somewhere.

Homer sneaked out of the house. To his astonishment, the burned-down barn was sitting there, big as life, with not a charred board on it.

Just as Homer was nearing the front gate, Pickey

stuck his head out the door. "How did you rest?" he wanted to know.

"Okay," said Homer.

"If you'll stick around, I'll play you a jig on the banjo," offered Pickey.

"Thanks, but I'll be getting on home," called Homer, running down the road as fast as he could. Then he remembered his manners. Still running, he called back, "I sure enjoyed my stay."

Strange All Through

No, I've never seen a ghost, but I can feel them. When a ghost is around, my hair rises up on my head and something touches me and I feel strange all through.

Emma Monroe
Tin City
Near Savannah

PRECAUTIONS TO TAKE
WHEN SOMEONE DIES

- *Give the deceased a proper burial, or his spirit will not be allowed into Heaven or Hell, and he will be doomed to walk the earth forever, looking for a final resting place.*
- *Cover all mirrors in the house immediately after a person has died, or you might see the person's spirit in the mirror.*
- *After the funeral you should empty all cups, pans, and buckets, because the spirit will remain in the house if there is water around.*
- *Change the house in some way. Move the doorknobs so the ghost cannot find its way in. Or put a new addition on the house to confuse the ghost.*

The Ghost of a Jealous Man

The first time I ever saw a ghost was long years back. Once when I was young and receiving company, there were two men coming to see me. I liked one man the best and the other man was jealous. Well, the jealous man died. After that many a time I saw a shadow like him come right up to my door and disappear. One night he came, stretched his arm across the door, and said just as plain as anything in a big loud voice, "Is that other man still coming around you?" I was scared stiff.

Chloe West
Currytown

HER HUSBAND'S GHOST

A unt Jessie Collins did not know what she had done to deserve the haunting.

When her husband died, she gave him a fine funeral. She went into deep mourning and wore a long, black widow's veil. She went to the cemetery every morning and cried all day at his grave.

"But his spirit started to haunt me something terrible," she explained. "I had chickens, and every night he'd come back wearing a white apron and shoo my chickens. Every morning some of them would be dead.

"Then I got mad and took off my widow's veil and stopped going to the cemetery. He didn't like that, so he started to drive my horse crazy.

"Finally I fixed that haunt. I sprinkled black pepper around the sills of all my doors. That stopped him. You know, that always chases ghosts."

CALVIN COPLEY AND THE WIDOW

A man died. His wife buried him in his Sunday best. He wore a blue suit, a white shirt, and white socks with a blue pattern in them. She put a red rose in the lapel of his suit. She did not put shoes on him.

The man was not in the ground more than a week or so when Calvin Copley, who worked at the church, started coming around to see the widow. A few days later, Calvin Copley was sweeping out the church, as was his custom.

Suddenly he saw a man walk through the church door. The man wore a blue suit and a white shirt. He had no shoes on, but wore socks with a blue pattern in them. In the lapel of his suit jacket was a red rose.

Before Calvin Copley even had time to be scared, the man turned around and walked back out of the church toward the cemetery.

Calvin Copley told everyone he saw about the ghost of the dead man, but while others tried, no one else ever saw him. Of course Calvin Copley was different from most other people, for he had been born with

a caul over his head. That made him far more likely to
see ghosts.

Needless to say, Calvin Copley stopped courting
the dead man's widow.

THE SATURDAY-NIGHT FIDDLER

During cotton-picking time in the Red River Bottoms of East Texas, Saturday is the day that the cotton pickers have themselves a real ball. They build themselves plank platforms on the farm where they are working and dance until the roosters start to crow for daytime Sunday morning.

The farmers can't hold the cotton pickers down either, or keep them from running away with things. They have a saying, "If a white man could be a black man in the Bottoms for just one Saturday night, he would never want to be a white man again."

They always have a fiddler to play the music for the dance, and he can always count on getting about twenty dollars for the night, and that's more than a schoolteacher makes in a couple of weeks. News travels around fast about the quick money that fiddlers make in the Red River Bottoms on a Saturday night, so fiddlers from every which where make their way into there. On occasion a fiddler even comes from way down in Louisiana, on the other side of the Red River, to play for these Saturday-night dances.

Once, one of these Louisiana fellows was late getting off from Shreveport and didn't land in the Bottoms until pitch dark. The reason it was way past dark when he reached the Bottoms was that he brought his little brother with him.

His mother had just died and left his little brother, and the fiddler was the only living relative the little boy had. The little boy had to tag along with the fiddler wherever he could latch onto a job playing the fiddle.

The fiddler worried a whole lot about getting to the Bottoms so late, because he had an extra mouth to feed now.

His pocket change was real low, and he didn't even know if he was going to get a job that night. It was getting late, and his little brother's feet were sore and his legs were aching. The fiddler didn't want the little boy to walk any farther, but where in the name of the Lord was he going to leave the little boy while he hunted for a place to play his fiddle?

He was wondering and wondering when just then he looked up and saw a white man jogging along the road on a saddle horse, and he stopped the white man and asked him if he knew where the cotton pickers were having a dance that Saturday night, and did he know a place where he could leave his little brother while he went looking for a place to fiddle? The white man told him that they were having a big dance a ways down the road on the left-hand side and that there was an old cottonseed house here on the right-hand side where he could leave his little brother. The fiddler thanked the man, then took a box of matches out of his pocket, lit one of them, and looked across the fence to the right; and sure enough, there was the cottonseed house just like the white man had told him. He was tickled to death to find a place to leave his little brother. So he took him by the hand and, holding his fiddle in the other, climbed through the fence and went over to the cottonseed house. There was a ladder leading to a window on one side, so he climbed up the ladder and carried the little boy through the window. He took the blankets he was carrying on his shoulder for himself and the little boy to sleep on, spread out one of them for the little boy, and gave him a paper sack with some cheese and crackers and ginger snaps in it in case he got hungry. He then took his fiddle, told his little brother, "So long," and struck out down the road to see if he could find the spot where they were having the dance.

The cottonseed was piled up so high in the cottonseed house that it almost reached the ceiling, and the little boy barely had room to stretch himself out, but finally he managed somehow to get himself fixed so he could lie down and rest his tired legs. But his brother hadn't been gone more than a couple of minutes when the little boy heard a puffing noise, and when he lifted his head up to see what the trouble was, what do you think he saw? Some smoke coming through the window of the little cottonseed house. The little boy was so scared that he pulled the blanket over his face real quick and started trembling like a leaf. He lay there for quite a while, until finally he got up enough courage to peek out from under the cover, and what do you think he saw this time? A great big white dog standing at the foot of his blanket looking down at him. The little boy was so scared, he couldn't even holler. He just lay there

wondering if the dog was going to move from where she was standing. But the dog just stood there and looked down at the little boy and didn't make a sound.

Finally the little boy saw that the dog didn't act like she was going to bite him, so he dozed off to sleep and slept about eight hours. When he woke up, it was about five o'clock in the morning, and the dog was still standing over him just like she was before he had gone to sleep. Pretty soon he heard his brother coming down the road playing his fiddle, and just before his brother reached the cottonseed house, the dog turned back into smoke again and went back out the window she'd come in. The little brother told the fiddler what happened, and the fiddler told him that the dog was their mother, who'd come back from the grave to keep watch over the little fellow while he was away fiddling for the cotton pickers' dance.

GHOSTS AND BURIED TREASURE

*I*t was said that when a slave owner buried a jar of treasure, he killed the most evil slave on his plantation so
that his spirit might keep watch over the jar. If the owner
never returned, the plat-eye spirit of the slave remained to
do vengeance to anyone who might disturb the treasure.
That is why such jars are often found with human bones
beside them or under them.

Sometimes guiding spirits inform living persons of hid-
den treasure and show them where to look for it.

But sometimes a plat-eye watches the treasure. The
plat-eye can take many animal forms, including a hunch-
back hog, a five-footed cow, and a double-headed dog. But
in South Carolina Sea Island lore, it is always chained to
a tree.

Of course, folks in the know can find that treasure by
understanding the habits of the plat-eye. One surefire way
is to listen for the sound of chains rattling in the night.
You can be sure that the noise is being made by a plat-eye
rubbing against a tree, trying to get the chain loose. Then
all a treasure hunter has to do is find the tree.

A TREASURE-HUNTING STORY

One warm summer evening an old black woman stepped out of her kitchen to the back porch to get a breath of fresh air and ran right into a white man.

"Hello, Sarah," the white man said. "I want you to meet me behind the milk house at eleven o'clock. I have something for you."

Sarah didn't answer him. She just opened her mouth and began to scream. She shrieked so loudly that all the other house servants ran out. Then Sarah told them she had met no one but the spirit of her former master, Mr. Mercier.

"It sure was him," Sarah vowed between yells and sobs of terror. "I'd of known him anywhere. He told me to meet him at eleven o'clock. Just before he vanished, he said he had gold buried behind that milk house. But I don't want a dead man's gold. I don't even want to see a dead man."

Gold! The others wanted to know more about it. In a day or two the news had spread all through the neighborhood. *Gold!* Even the group's preacher became excited,

and finally it was he who led them on a treasure hunt.

They met behind the milk house one night, and the preacher took a shovel and began to dig. All of a sudden, as the preacher worked away with his shovel, he began to yell. He dropped the shovel and sprawled face downward on the earth, crying louder and louder, screaming that the Devil had him and that he was dying. The bystanders could hear the sound of a whip lashing through the air, could see the preacher's shirt darken with blood.

Sarah came running up and fought her way through the crowd. She shrieked, "Mr. Mercier is whipping the preacher! I can see him! He's mad because you all went after his gold, and he's whipping the Reverend." No one else could see who was doing the whipping, but they could all see the preacher, now moaning and writhing on the ground.

A few days later the Reverend died from the effects of the beating.

THE HEADLESS HAUNT

A man and his wife were traveling along a muddy road on a cold, rainy night. It was pitch-dark, and they were tired and hungry, but they could not find a place to stop for the night.

Then, through the mists, they saw a large house, with smoke coming from the chimney and a fire flickering on the windowpanes. They went around to the back door and knocked, hoping to ask for a little food and some shelter.

"Come in," said a voice. They went in. They looked around to see who the voice belonged to, but they couldn't see anyone.

There was a pot of beans simmering, and a stew boiling in another pot. The couple knew it was somebody else's supper. But it was so warm by the fire, they decided the owner wouldn't mind if they warmed themselves a bit.

Then they decided it would be all right if they made themselves some coffee. The husband took a bucket and went off to find the spring, while the woman took off her shoes and socks and warmed her feet at the fire.

Suddenly, a man walked right through the closed door. The wife knew it was a man because he had on shoes and pants and a vest and a coat and a shirt and a collar. But he didn't have a head! There was nothing above the bloody stump of his neck.

"What do you want?" asked the woman, shivering now with fear, not cold.

"I am miserable," said the headless man, speaking from a mouth that wasn't there. "I need my head."

"Where is it?" the woman wanted to know.

Just then her husband came back with the pail of spring water. When he saw the headless haunt, he practically jumped out of his skin. But his wife told him that the man was just about to explain how he got that way.

"I was killed by two men," the headless haunt began. "They cut off my head and took my head and my body to the cellar and buried me in two places. They killed me for my money, but they didn't get it. They looked everywhere, they dug up the cellar, but they didn't find the money. They went away, leaving me buried in two pieces."

Then the man said, "If you come to the cellar with me and find my head and bury me all in one grave, I'll make you rich."

The couple agreed to help him. "If we're going down to the cellar, we need a torch," said the husband.

"No need for a torch," said the headless haunt. He stuck his finger into the fire, and it blazed up like a pine knot. Holding his flaming finger high, the haunt led the way down the steps to the cellar.

Once they had got used to the semidarkness, the couple could see the large hole where the headless haunt had been buried. A shovel was still lying where the robbers had left it. "Take that shovel and dig over there," said the headless haunt. "That is where I buried my barrels of gold and money."

The husband picked up the shovel and dug, and soon the shovel struck something with a thud. A little more digging, and the husband was able to lift a heavy barrel out of the dirt. A little more digging, and he found the other.

"You are rich," said the headless haunt. "Now find my head. Dig over there."

The husband dug where he was told. Soon he had unearthed the head. Not wanting to touch it, he lifted it up in the shovel. The headless haunt reached over, plucked the head from the shovel, and put it on his bloody neck. Then he took off his burning finger and stuck it in the candlestick. Finally, holding his head on with one hand, he used the other to crawl back into the

hole he had come out of. The husband shoveled dirt over him.

The last thing the couple heard the man say was "You can have my money. You can have my house and land. Thank you for burying me in one piece."

The couple lived there happily ever after.

I Don't Want to Fool
With No Spirits

I see spirits all the time. They are little and white and have no head. You don't bother them none and they leave you alone.

There used to be an old house right past ours. Every night we would be woken up by a loud banging noise. If we looked out the window, we could see this spirit. He was always wandering around. Every now and then he would throw a rock at a gasoline tank, and it would make that noise we heard. We always used to think there was buried treasure near and this spirit was guarding it. I never did look for the treasure—I don't want to fool with no spirits. After a time they took down the house, and the spirit never came back anymore.

Stephen Bryant
Springfield

THE GIRL AND THE PLAT-EYE

One night in a coastal area of the South a young girl went out clamming, but the tide was very late going out, and she was very late setting off for home. As she came to a small log bridge, she saw in front of her a huge black cat.

Its eyes were like balls of fire, and its back was arched. Its tail twitched back and forth, and its hair stood on end. It walked across the log in front of her.

The girl said out loud, "I'm not afraid. That ain't no ghost. Ain't no plat-eye. Ain't no nuthin'!"

Then the huge black cat turned around and started toward her.

The girl raised her short clam rake and brought it down, as hard as she could, across the animal's back. If it had been a real cat, she would have pinned it to the log. But the rake went right through it. The cat rose up on its hind legs and pawed the air.

The girl took off in the other direction.

After running awhile, she had to stop for breath. "Thank you, Lord, for delivering me from that cat,"

she began, and then she saw the cat. It was as big as a cow, and its eyes burned into her.

She took off again. Just before she reached a clearing, the cat jumped in front of her. This time it was as big as an ox. Suddenly it vanished behind a tree.

The girl's uncle Murphy was a witch doctor. When she told him about the plat-eye in the woods, he gave her some advice: "When you travel in the deep woods where the moss wave low, where Mr. Cooter live and Mr. Moccasin crawl, and the firefly flicker, you carry sulfur and gunpowder mixed in your pocket. Plat-eye can't stand them smells mixed."

From then on, the girl never traveled in the woods at night without loading her pockets with that special mixture, and she never saw a plat-eye again.

THE HALF-CLAD GHOST

There once was an old man who always wore two pairs of drawers. But when he died, his wife laid out only one pair for him. After the funeral, he kept coming back and coming back. Every night he'd come right in the front door of her house. So she moved from that place, but he just kept coming. She moved four or five times, and he just kept coming back every night. Finally, she talked to some of her friends. They asked her why she didn't talk to him. She said she was afraid to. But they told her to say, "What in the name of the Lord do you want?" So that night he came again.

This time she walked right up to him and said, "What in the name of the Lord do you want?"

He looked at her for a long time, but she never moved, just stood there. Finally he said, "Honey, give me another pair of drawers please."

She said, "All right, I'll give them to you," and from that day to this he has never come back.

That's the way it is. When you ask them what in the name of the Lord they want, and then tell them you'll give it to them, they'll go away and leave you alone. You don't actually have to give it, just agree to.

The Spirit of a Friend

I always knew there were witches and ghosts. After I got married, my husband told me that he sees a ghost. He described the ghost to me. It wasn't long before I was seeing the ghost too. Sometimes he would say to me, "There goes the spirit. It's just floating along, ain't got no head." Sure enough, there I would see a shadow floating by me.

Sometimes my husband saw the spirit of some friend of ours. That was a sure sign that something was going to happen to that person, either sickness or death. One day he saw a ghost of a close friend of his. The next day he got a telegram that said the friend was dead.

Dorothy Johnson
Springfield

JACK-O'-LANTERN TALES

Today when you say jack-o'-lantern, people think about Halloween and pumpkins. In folklore, a jack-o'-lantern is the evil spirit of a person who was not allowed into either Heaven or Hell.

Those who have seen a jack-o'-lantern describe it as a large, hairy creature with goggle eyes and a huge mouth. They say it bounds along like a human-size grasshopper. But most do not see them, only the lights they carry. You can watch the light bob up and down as the jack-o'-lantern walks to and fro, looking for people to lead astray.

HOW JACK BECAME A
JACK-O'-LANTERN

Jack wanted power, and he knew how to get it. All he
had to do was go to the crossroads at midnight and
sell himself to the Devil.

One night Jack went to the crossroads. When midnight came, so did the Devil.

"Devil," said Jack, "I hear you will give me all the
power I want."

"Yes, Jack," said the Devil. "For seven years you will
have all the power you want. But after that time your
soul will belong to me."

Jack figured he had seven years to come up with a
way to outsmart the Devil. He said, "Devil, you got
yourself a deal."

For the next seven years Jack had all the power he
wanted. As the end of the time approached, he started
thinking about how to keep the power and keep his
soul, too. When the Devil came to claim Jack's soul,
Jack was ready for him.

"Jack, I've come for your soul," said the Devil.

"Okay," said Jack. "But first will you get that piece of shoe sole from above the door for me?"

The Devil didn't see why Jack couldn't get it himself, but he was willing to grant this last wish of Jack's. The Devil reached for the piece of shoe sole.

Just then Jack sprang into action. He took a hammer and nailed the Devil's hand to the door.

Poor old Satan hung by his hand nailed to the door. It was very painful. "Let me go," he pleaded.

"Only if you promise not to take my soul," said Jack.

"Okay, keep your soul. Just let me go."

The Devil did not bother Jack again for the rest of his life.

When Jack died, he went up to Heaven. But he was not allowed in. He went down to Hell, but the Devil was waiting for him. The Devil threw a chunk of fire at him and told him he was too smart for Hell.

Jack picked up the chunk of fire to light his way and wandered off. He wanders still, in the swamps and forests, angry that he can find no resting place and determined to lure unsuspecting people into trouble.

THE END OF HOCK

Hock and Old Man Lunnen were walking along the road one night when they saw a light moving through the marsh.

Hock said, "I'm going to see what that is."

Old Man Lunnen told him to stay on the road. "You don't know what's out there," he warned.

Hock said he wasn't scared, and he was going to see what it was. Old Man Lunnen said he wasn't going to have anything to do with it.

Next thing Old Man Lunnen knew, Hock was falling down holes and scrambling in the briars and acting like he was possessed. Then Hock disappeared altogether.

When Hock didn't come home after a few hours, Old Man Lunnen went and got a search party. They found Hock later that night. He was standing knee deep in mud, his head reared back and his hands sticking out in front of him. His eyes were wide open and his mouth was twisted in terror. And he was stone cold dead, frightened to death by a jack-o'-lantern.

The Ghost in the Stetson

I've seen ghosts all my life. Once it was just after my father died. I saw him all dressed up and wearing a Stetson hat. I called my mother and said, "Mother, here comes Papa." When I turned around, he was gone.

After I got married, I moved out by the water tanks. A friend of mine named Arthur Perry died. Some time later another friend died. One night I was lying down when I heard a noise. I looked up and there were those two men all dressed up in white, walking across that room. As I watched them, they began to shrink until they were no bigger than dolls. Then they disappeared. I see ghosts most anytime, so I'm used to it now.

Henry Higgens
Brownville

HOLD HIM, TABB

A group of horse-drawn freight wagons was traveling together from town to town one cold December.

One afternoon it began to snow, and the drivers decided not to try to go much farther. They continued on until they could find a place to pull over and camp. That place turned out to be an abandoned farm. The men unhitched their horses and put them in the stalls in the barn. Then they turned toward the house, thinking they could stay inside it.

About that time, a man came along. He said he was the owner of the farm and that they were welcome to stay there. But he warned, "You won't want to stay in that house. It's haunted. Nobody has stayed in it and lived to tell about it for twenty-five years."

On hearing that warning, the drivers decided it wasn't such a good idea to camp out at the farm. They hitched their horses back up and moved up the road about a half mile, where there was a stand of trees that would afford them some shelter. All the drivers except one, that is.

The driver named Tabb announced, "I'm not afraid of any haunts. And I'm not moving myself or my horses outside to spend the night in the snow. I'm staying where I am."

So Tabb moved into the house. He built a big fire in the fireplace. He unpacked his food and cooked himself a nice meal. Then he unrolled his bedroll and stretched it out by the fire and got into bed and went to sleep.

Around dawn he woke up, rested and warm. He thought about the other drivers, who must have spent the night shivering in the snow. "What fools those other fellows are to be afraid to stay here," he said to himself. "This place isn't even haunted." But then he looked up at the ceiling, and his eyes grew very wide.

A ghost was on the ceiling—a man dressed in white, lying as flat against the ceiling as you would against the floor. For a moment Tabb thought the ghost was stuck to the ceiling. But then it fell on top of him!

"Get off me!" cried Tabb as he struggled to get out from under the ghost. But the ghost would not let go. They rolled around and around on the floor, crashing into furniture. A half mile away, the other drivers heard the commotion and rushed to the house. They peered in through the window.

At that moment, Tabb was on top. "Hold him, Tabb, hold him!" they cried.

"I got him!" Tabb yelled back.

But the ghost also had hold of Tabb. It leaped into the air, and before anyone knew what had happened, it had Tabb up on the roof.

Tabb held on. "Hold him, Tabb, hold him!" screamed the men.

"You bet your boots I got him," Tabb yelled down from the roof.

Then the ghost made a great leap into the air. The drivers watched as Tabb and the ghost sailed off into nowhere, and heard his last cry: "I got him, and he got me, too!"

CIVIL WAR GHOSTS

The Civil War was a defining event for the American South. For five years the Rebels who had seceded from the Union, and formed the Confederate States of America, fought to preserve slavery and the "Southern way of life" against the Yankees who were determined to keep the Union intact. By the time the Confederate forces surrendered, much of the region had been devastated, and hundreds of thousands of young Southerners had lost their lives. Nearly every Southern town has a monument to its fallen heroes and a body of stories from the war. There are many Civil War ghost stories, especially centering around the battlefields where so many young men died.

THE GHOSTS OF CEDAR CREEK

Cedar Creek, Virginia, was the scene of a major Civil War battle. In nearby Middletown, the Episcopal church served as a practice hall for the army band. It also served as a hospital during the battle. Many wounded soldiers died in there and were buried in the churchyard. But they did not remain there long.

After the war, the bodies of the soldiers were dug up and placed in simple pine coffins. These were stacked up against the church wall to await shipment by train to the soldiers' families. The boxes stayed stacked up like that for close to a month.

According to one former slave who lived on his master's farm on the edge of Middletown, one night a light came out of the church and moved directly to the pile of coffins, as if an invisible person was searching around with a candle.

Another night, an animal resembling a calf came out of the church and walked around the churchyard.

The coffins were eventually taken away, but the souls of the soldiers had been disturbed in their resting

places. They did not go away. Local people often heard them moaning and groaning in the church or church-yard.

On some dark nights, the sounds of a band could be heard coming from the church.

The battlefield, too, was thick with ghosts. It was not uncommon to hear shooting and the sound of gal-loping horses. More than one person walking near the battlefield at night insisted that a horse had ridden right up to them, although it could not be seen.

THE GHOST OF
THE YANKEE SOLDIER

There was one particular ghost that haunted a barn down by Cedar Creek. He wore a Yankee uniform and high cavalry boots that came up over his knees. Some people said he was headless, but others said he not only had his head but also wore a hat.

The first person who ever saw him was a farmer named Holt Hottel, who had rented the farm. Hottel went out to feed his horses one night just after sundown. He went up into the hayloft and was about to throw a pitchfork full of hay down into the feeding hole when he saw what he thought was a tramp on the stairs.

"Get out of here," he said. "I don't allow tramps in the barn on account of fire."

There was no answer.

Then Hottel struck at the "tramp" with his pitchfork. The fork went right through him and into the barn boards. Hottel realized this was not a tramp. He jumped down the hole into the feeding room and

hightailed it to the house.

After a while, Hottel got used to seeing the ghost. He never did him any harm. In fact, he never did anything but stand on the steps.

Once Hottel even spent the whole night in the barn. He did so to guard the wheat he had just harvested, fearing that it might be stolen. He went to sleep with the ghost standing on the hayloft steps.

The ghost of the Yankee soldier was seen by most people only at dusk. At that time, he would walk out of the hayloft and partway down the steps of the loft. He would just stand there looking.

Word about the ghost got around, and many people traveled to the barn just to get a glimpse of him. In fact, at one time the railroad ran excursion trains so people could see the ghost. But usually he did not appear to them. There were some people who tried for nights on end to see him and never did, and other people who saw him even though they weren't looking for him.

The old folks said that the people who couldn't see ghosts only saw steam.

THE GHOST OF A MAN
THE YANKEES KILLED

During the Civil War a Southerner named Old Man Cook was killed by Yankees near Bono, Arkansas.

One evening not long afterward, a black man named Suggs went to a creek near the site to get some water. When he got to the creek, he saw a big old dog sitting on the embankment.

"Get away from here, dog," yelled Suggs. When the dog refused to move, Suggs threw his bucket at it. The bucket went clean through the dog.

"It's a ghost!" said Suggs to himself as he ran for his life, leaving his bucket behind him.

Word got around about what Suggs had seen.

"That spot where Suggs saw the ghost dog is right about where the Yankees killed Old Man Cook," the people said to each other.

Most of them stayed away from that spot at night. But some brave people went there trying to see the dog.

Some saw the dog. Others saw a cat. At least one person saw a rooster a foot and a half tall. All agreed that whatever form it took, it was guarding the spot where Old Man Cook had been killed by the Yankees.

I See Spirits

Iwas birthed with my wisdom because I was the seventh child and born with a caul.

I see spirits. There is a little ghost that stays right around this house. The first night I moved in here, he walked right in and jumped on me. I managed to throw him off. Now he comes every night. Sometimes he stands at the gate with his feet high off the ground and his face turned backward, but he can always see you. I don't talk to him any or try to come close, because he would harm me or cause me to harm myself. I just pass him by as if he wasn't there. But I see him.

I know there must be buried treasure where this house is built, for wherever there is money or other treasure, a ghost is put there to guard it. One time I went out to Deptford with two other men to dig up a pot of money that I knew was buried there. I saw three spirits, one man and two women. We dug and dug, and finally we could see the pot of money. Just then one of the women laughed, "Ha! Ha! Ha!" The pot sunk down deeper in the ground. We all ran.

The laugh that spirit gave went right through me. I never tried to dig up the money again. Right now I know there is treasure buried here under me, but I wouldn't try to get it. It is bad luck. That spirit warned me.

Nathaniel Lewis
Tin City
Near Savannah

DEAD AARON

Aaron Kelly died, so they buried him. That night the mourners were sitting around the fire.

His widow was saying, "I hope he's gone, but I suspect he isn't," when in walked the corpse.

The corpse sat down between his widow and the lead mourner and said, "What's this all about? You all act like somebody's dead. Who's dead?"

"You are," said the widow, shaking like a leaf.

"Me dead?" said Aaron Kelly. "How come? I don't feel dead."

The others told him, "You don't feel dead, but you look dead, Aaron. You better go back to the grave where you belong."

"No," said Aaron. "I'm not going back to any grave until I feel dead." With that, he moved closer to the fire and started trying to warm his hands and feet, all the while giving a chill to the room that hadn't been there before. That's all he did, night and day, was sit by the fire.

Well, that sure presented a problem. For one thing, Aaron Kelly sure looked dead. His joints cracked, his skin looked dusty. His widow and the other mourners weren't sure how long the corpse was going to last. But that was just part of the problem. The insurance association wouldn't pay on his life insurance policy because Aaron swore he wasn't dead. And the undertaker said he was going to take back the coffin if Aaron wasn't going to occupy it.

Aaron's widow tried to explain all this to Aaron, but he wouldn't listen. "Let me be, woman!" he said. "I'm not going back to any burying ground until I'm dead. Don't you miss me?"

"Miss you?" she wanted to know. "How am I going to miss you? I haven't had a chance to miss you. You're not gone."

"Aren't you going to mourn for me?" Aaron next wanted to know.

She replied, "What's the use of going into mourning when I haven't lost you yet?"

"You haven't paid proper attention to me," he charged.

"Haven't paid proper attention?" she wanted to know. "Didn't we take you out and bury you? Didn't the Reverend preach the funeral? You think we're going to bury you two times? Well, we aren't. So quit complaining."

Aaron just sat by the fire and creaked and cracked. His joints were dry, his back was stiff, and every time he moved, he cracked and creaked like a dead tree in the wind.

One night the best fiddler in town came to court the widow. He sat on one side of the fire, and Aaron sat on the other, trying to warm his hands and feet and creaking and cracking. The fiddler grew tired of hearing Aaron creak and crack. The widow was tired of the whole situation.

"How long do we have to put up with this dead corpse?" she wanted to know. "How long do we have to wait until he molders? How long do we have to sit by our own fire, you, and me, and *him*?"

But the fiddler didn't have any answers.

By and by Aaron Kelly rose and stretched and said, "This isn't much fun. Let's have some fun. Let's dance to limber up our legs."

So the fiddler got out his fiddle and began to play, and Aaron got up to dance. He shook himself. He took a step or two. He began to do a jig, with his old bones cracking and his yellow teeth snapping, his knee bones knocking, and his arms flip-flopping, around and around and around. He skipped and he pranced, and how that dead man could dance!

Pretty soon a piece of him flew loose and fell to the floor.

"My golly, look at that!" said the fiddler.

"Play faster!" cried the widow.

The fiddler played faster. Dead Aaron danced faster, and pieces of bone kept popping and dropping every which way. With every hop a dry bone dropped.

"Oh, my God!" cried the fiddler.

"Play, man, play!" hollered the widow.

The fiddler played faster. Dead Aaron danced faster, bones dropping all around, until all at once he crumbled down, and there Dead Aaron lay, just a heap of bones on the floor, except for the bald head, which danced by itself, grinning at the fiddler.

"Play faster yet!" cried the widow. But the fiddler wasn't interested in playing for a grinning, dancing skull.

"Widow, I've got to go get me some more rosin for my bow," he said, and he took off running.

They gathered the bones together and put them

back in the grave. But they were careful to lay the bones one across the other and all confused, so Aaron couldn't figure out how they went back together. After that, Dead Aaron didn't get up out of the grave anymore.

The widow remained a widow from that day on, though. That dancing head spoiled her chances for romance.

PROTECTION AGAINST GHOSTS, SPIRITS, AND HAUNTS

- *Wear your coat inside out when you travel at night or go to an area that is haunted.*
- *Have water close by when you go to bed at night. That way, if your dream soul gets thirsty, the water is right there. If there is no water, your dream soul won't let you rest.*
- *Pull your pockets inside out.*
- *Carry a new knife that has never cut wood.*
- *Carry a mixture of sulfur and gunpowder in your pocket.*

But it is wise not to depend too much on any form of protection against ghosts.

AUTHOR'S NOTES

The ideas and beliefs revealed by these stories and ghostly experiences can be traced in some instances to specific cultures. The idea that a baby born with a caul would be able to see ghosts was found both in West Africa and in England. In some areas the practice was to remove the caul, dry it, grind it into a powder, and feed it to the infant two or three days after it was born.

The notion that a person born on Christmas Day could see ghosts is an African one. In England it was believed that a person born on Christmas could *not* see ghosts.

Plat-eye ghosts are found in American folklore only among African Americans. African folklore includes a bad spirit that has an eye in the center of its forehead and webbed feet like a duck. It wanders restlessly through the night. The African-American version of this spirit is a plat-eye.

West Indian folklore contains many plat-eye stories. The plat-eye frequently has one eye that dangles from the middle of its forehead. The word plait, often pronounced "plat," can refer to a braid of hair, and perhaps plat-eye refers to one eye hanging from a thread.

In the folklore of the South Carolina Sea Islands, plat-eyes are assigned to guard buried treasure. As such, they are probably relatives of African spirits that guard buried treasure. A similar belief has been found in Haiti. African-American folklore is filled with stories of buried treasure and the spirits that guard it. These stories have a strong basis in fact.

During the Civil War, Southerners in the path of oncoming Yankee forces would bury their valuables so the Yankees could not get them. Often it was the slaves who were commanded to bury them.

After the war ended, much of this buried treasure remained buried. Its original owners had either died or gone away. The slaves who had buried it had died or gone north to freedom.

———

African-American beliefs in jack-o'-lanterns are a combination of English, Scots-Irish, and African folklore. In Irish tradition the jack-o'-lantern is the spirit of a dead person who was not allowed into either Heaven or Hell. African Americans related that idea to the African belief that a body not given a proper burial was doomed to roam the earth looking for its home.

Like plat-eyes, jack-o'-lanterns are often seen in wooded or marshy places at night. That is because these are places where decaying timber can be found. At night decaying timber gives off a kind of glow that people call foxfire or foolish fire, which can easily be mistaken for the glow of a ghostly lantern.

———•·•———

Funerals and other rituals surrounding death were important to many cultures. In some areas of West Africa, a family would spend all its money and even go into debt in order to pay for a lavish funeral.

Not just a lavish funeral was expected, but also proper attention to the grave. In parts of Zaire and Angola, even today, broken dishes are used to decorate graves. This was also the practice during the time of New World slavery. The dishes were for the spirit to eat from. Only broken dishes were used because unbroken plates would be stolen. This same practice was observed by folklorist Newbell Niles Puckett earlier in this century in South Carolina, Mississippi, and Alabama.

Because they could afford lavish funerals, the

wealthy paid even more attention to proper burial of the dead. Large funerals were expected in colonial Boston, for example, and a mourning gift, such as a gold ring, was given to each mourner. One man wrote of having a tankard (a large mug) filled with gold mourning rings. Widows spent so much money on funerals that they had nothing left over to live on. This practice got so out of hand that the colonial authorities passed a law forbidding such costly funerals. But custom overshadowed law, and most people ignored the legal prohibition.

The idea of what constituted a proper funeral was much simpler in African-American culture. Slaves had no way of accumulating the wealth needed for costly funerals. Nor did most African Americans even after slavery. Here is what an old woman in Georgia in the 1930s had to say about what constituted acceptable practice after a death: "When a person dies in the house, if you take them out before the minister says a few words, then their spirit will haunt the house, because they just can't be happy until they have everything done proper and right."

In colonial America, among poor and working-class European settlers especially, it was the custom to build small cottages with door posts or witch posts to one side of the hearth. Sometimes these posts were carved with fertility symbols, angels, or other images of protection. Sometimes there were no posts but pins were stuck in doorframes. Although these symbols were most often found in the homes of the poor, just about everyone believed in some form of magic.

———————

Thanks to the Georgia Writers' Project of the 1930s, we have a record of early African-American beliefs in ghosts and spirits. The Georgia Writers' Project was part of the Works Progress Administration (WPA) created by President Franklin Delano Roosevelt. The WPA's purpose was to put people back to work during the Great Depression, and it sponsored projects for manual laborers and for artists and writers as well. In many areas WPA Writers' Projects wrote travel guides and collected local lore.

The Savannah Unit of the Georgia Writers' Project interviewed blacks in the state and tried to show that many of the beliefs and stories they heard could be traced directly to African beliefs and stories. Most of the black people interviewed were elderly and uneducated. Most of the WPA interviewers were white and not trained in writing in dialect. The interviews are difficult to read, so the selections included are not written in dialect. A collection of these interviews was published under the title *Drums and Shadows: Survival Studies Among the Georgia Coastal Negroes.*

When asked why they thought belief in ghosts was declining, some of the elderly people interviewed by WPA writers said that one reason was the Christian religion. The more religious people are, the less they believe in ghosts. Their fears about the unknown are diminished by a belief in a God who controls what happens in the world.

Another reason cited was progress. In the case of the Civil War ghosts near the site of the old Cedar Creek battlefield, old-timers explained that the land had been plowed up too much, disturbing the ghosts and driving them away.

SOURCES

"Wait Till Emmett Comes" adapted from The American Folklore Society, Ohio Joint Program in the Arts and Humanities, Columbus, Ohio.

"The Deserted Village" by Martha Eammons. Texas Folklore Society.

"Little Nero and the Magic Tea Cakes" adapted from J. Mason Brewer, *American Negro Folklore*, Chicago: Quadrangle Books, 1968.

"The Ghost Log Cabin" adapted from J. Mason Brewer, *American Negro Folklore*, Chicago: Quadrangle Books, 1968.

"Uncle Henry and the Dog Ghost" adapted from J. Mason Brewer, *American Negro Folklore*, Chicago: Quadrangle Books, 1968.

"Daddy and the Plat-Eye Ghost" from Eleanora E. Tate, *The Secret of Gumbo Grove*, New York: Franklin Watts, Inc., 1987.

"Two Boys and a Plat-Eye" adapted from Julia A. Peterkin and Doris Ullmann, *Roll, Jordan, Roll*, New York: Robert O. Ballou, 1933.

"A Night at Pickey's" adapted from W. C. Hendricks, ed., *Bundle of Troubles and Other Tarheel Tales*, Durham, NC: Duke

University Press, 1943.

"Her Husband's Ghost" in Langston Hughes and Arna Bontemps, *The Book of Negro Folklore*, New York: Dodd, Mead & Company, 1958.

"Calvin Copley and the Widow" adapted from Richard M. Dorson, *American Negro Folktales*, Greenwich, CT: Fawcett Publications, 1967.

"The Saturday-Night Fiddler" adapted from J. Mason Brewer, *American Negro Folklore*, Chicago: Quadrangle Books, 1968.

"A Treasure-Hunting Story" adapted from Lyle Saxon et al. (Louisiana Writers' Project), *Gumbo Ya-Ya*, Boston and New York: Houghton Mifflin, 1945.

"The Headless Haunt" adapted from W. C. Hendricks, ed., *Bundle of Troubles and Other Tarheel Tales*, Durham, NC: Duke University Press, 1943.

"The Girl and the Plat-Eye" adapted from Writers' Program, Works Progress Administration, *South Carolina Folk Tales: Stories of Animals and Supernatural Beings*, Columbia, SC: University of South Carolina Press, 1941.

"The Half-Clad Ghost" by Martha Eammons. Texas Folklore Society.

"How Jack Became a Jack-o'-Lantern" adapted from Newbell Niles Puckett, *Folk Beliefs of the Southern Negro*, Montclair, NJ: Patterson Press, 1926, reprinted by Patterson Smith Publishing Co, 1968.

"The End of Hock" adapted from E.C.L. Adams, "Jack-Ma-Lantern" in *Congaree Sketches*, Chapel Hill, NC: University of North Carolina Press, 1927, reprinted 1987. Used with the permission of Stephen B. Adams and Adaline H. Adams.

"Hold Him, Tabb" from *Southern Workman and Hampton School Record*, June 1897, Vol. 26, No. 6, pp. 122–123.

Stories of battlefield ghosts adapted from Clifton Johnson, *Battleground Adventures: The Stories of Dwellers on the Scenes of Conflict in Some of the Most Notable Battles of the Civil War*, Boston and New York: Houghton Mifflin, 1915.

"Dead Aaron" adapted from "Dead Aaron II" as told by Sarah Rutledge and Epsie Meggets, from John Bennett, *The Doctor to the Dead: Grotesque Legends and Folk Tales of Old Charleston*, New York: Rinehart & Co., Inc., 1943.

All personal ghostly experiences are from *Drums and Shadows: Survival Studies Among Georgia Coastal Negroes*. Savannah Unit, Georgia Writers' Project, Works Progress Administration. Westport, CT: Greenwood Press, 1941; reprinted, 1973.

ADDITIONAL SOURCES

Abrahams, Roger D., ed. *Afro-American Folktales*. New York: Pantheon Books, Inc., 1985.

Boles, John B. *Black Southerners 1619–1869*. Lexington, KY: University Press of Kentucky, 1983.

Botkin, B. A., ed. *A Treasury of Southern Folklore*. New York: Bonanza Books, 1977; reprinted 1980.

Coffin, Tristram Potter, and Hennig Cohen, eds. *Folklore from the Working Folk of America*. Garden City, NY: Doubleday & Company, Inc., 1973.

Genovese, Eugene D. *Roll, Jordan, Roll: The World the Slaves Made*. New York: Vintage Books, 1976.

Goss, Linda, and Marian Barnes, eds. *Talk That Talk: An Anthology of African-American Storytelling*. New York: Simon & Schuster, Inc., 1989.

Jagendorf, M. A. *Folk Stories of the South.* New York: Vanguard Press, 1972.

Lyons, Mary E., ed. *Raw Head, Bloody Bones: African-American Tales of the Supernatural.* New York: Charles Scribner's Sons, 1991.

Parsons, Elsie Clews. *Folk-Lore of the Sea Islands, South Carolina.* Chicago: Afro-Am Press, 1969.

Sobel, Mechal. *The World They Made Together: Black and White Values in Eighteenth-Century Virginia.* Princeton, NJ: Princeton University Press, 1987.